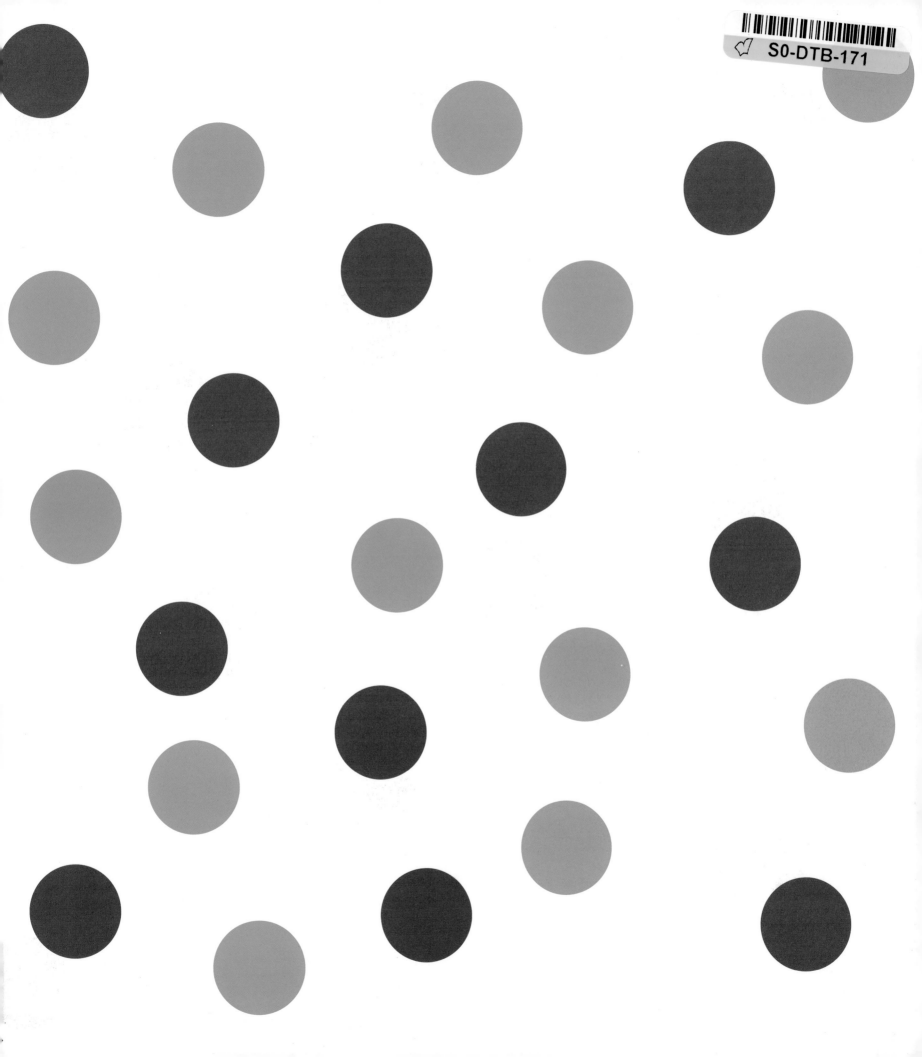

MY
COOK
BOOK

MY
COOK
BOOK

Caroline Green

For Kids

Western Publishing Company, Inc.
Racine, Wisconsin 53404

CREDITS

Managing editor: Veronica Ross
Art director: Rachael Stone
Home economist: Penny Morris
Photographer: Jonathan Pollock
Assistant photographer: Peter Cassidy
Editor: Joanna Dickens
Designer: Anita Ruddell
Illustrator: Tony Randell
Character illustrator: Jo Gapper
Typeset by: SX Composing Ltd, Rayleigh, Essex
Color separation by: P & W Graphics, Pte., Singapore

CONTENTS

INTRODUCTION

My Cook Book is the perfect introduction to cooking for beginners. All sorts of delicious recipes are included, each one with easy-to-follow instructions and colorful step-by-step pictures to help you. Learn how to make easy party jelly tarts, or tasty tandoori chicken for a main meal. There is also a section to show you how to make a three-course meal for friends or family.

BEFORE YOU BEGIN
- Read the instructions before you begin.
- Gather together all the ingredients you need.
- Protect your clothes with an apron.

WHEN YOU HAVE FINISHED
- Wash all the utensils and put them away.
- Wipe clean the work surfaces.
- Put away all the ingredients.

CLEAN AND HEALTHY
Microscopic bacteria are all around us. Many are quite safe, but some are harmful and can cause food poisoning. To avoid getting stomach upsets, it is important to keep everything very clean. So please follow these simple rules:
- Wash your hands before you handle any food.
- Wear an apron and tie back long hair.
- Keep work surfaces and sink clean.
- Clean chopping boards thoroughly. If you can, use a separate board for chopping raw meat or chicken.
- Wash fruit and vegetables, and clear away rubbish and peelings.

SAFETY FIRST
Never cook anything unless there is an adult around to help you. Look out for the SAFETY TIP. It will appear on those recipes where you will need to ask an adult for help. The kitchen can be a dangerous place, so remember the basic rules of safety:
- Ask an adult to switch on the oven for you and make sure it is switched off when you have finished cooking.
- Always use oven gloves to put things into or take them out of the oven, or before picking up anything hot.

- Never leave the kitchen when something is cooking on the stove top.
- Turn saucepan handles toward the sides of the stove so that the pans cannot be knocked over accidentally.
- Do not touch electrical plugs and switches with wet hands.
- Be very careful when using sharp knives. Always cut on a chopping board and hold the knife so that the blade is pointing downward.

GROWN-UPS TAKE NOTE

Every recipe in *My Cook Book* has been created with simplicity yet effectiveness in mind. However, some potentially dangerous items such as sharp knives and ovens do need to be used. Obviously, your involvement will depend on the age and ability of your child, but we do recommend that you supervise young children when they are cooking.

MEASURING INGREDIENTS

It is very important to weigh or measure all the ingredients as accurately as possible, using kitchen scales and cup measures.

COOKING TERMS

Throughout the recipes we have used various cooking terms. As a beginner, you may not be familiar with all of them, so here is a list of ones we have used, with helpful comments to describe each one.

Boil Heat liquid in a saucepan until it bubbles quickly.

Cream together Beat sugar and butter together to form a pale creamy mixture when making cakes.

Fold in Mix ingredients very lightly, using a metal spoon and cutting into the mixture rather than stirring around and around.

Garnish Decorate food with something edible to make it look attractive.

Glaze Brush the surface of food with beaten egg or milk, before baking, to give it a shiny cooked surface and to help it brown.

Knead Work a mixture of flour and fat or liquid with your hands.

Rub in Rub softened fat into flour lightly with your fingertips.

Seasoning Add flavoring to recipes to bring out the taste of the food— usually small amounts of salt, pepper, herbs, or spices.

Separate (eggs) Divide the egg yolk from the egg white. To do this, tap the eggshell on the side of a bowl to crack it. Tip the egg into the bowl and then carefully lift the yolk out, using a slotted spoon, and put it in another bowl.

Sift Pass either a liquid, a powder, or a solid ingredient through a fine-meshed sieve to get rid of solid lumps.

Simmer Cook liquids gently just below boiling point.

Whisk Beat egg whites or cream very hard to add air to the mixture and make it light and fluffy. You can do this with a hand (balloon) whisk or rotary beater.

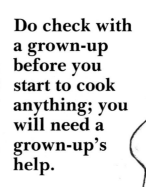

Do check with a grown-up before you start to cook anything; you will need a grown-up's help.

HEALTHFUL EATING

To help us grow strong and tall, keep warm, and heal when we are ill, we need fuel in the form of food and drink, just as a car needs gas in order to run. Food is made up of lots of different nutrients (healthful ingredients). The main ones are protein, carbohydrates, fat, vitamins, and minerals. We need a combination of these nutrients to keep us healthy, fit, and active. If we eat a well-balanced diet with a wide variety of different foods, we should get all the nutrients we need.

PROTEIN
Protein is used for growth and for repair of muscles, hair, blood, and skin. Most foods contain some protein, but meat, fish, milk, beans, cereals, and nuts are the most concentrated forms. It is very important to eat some of these foods every day.

CARBOHYDRATES
Carbohydrates are our main source of energy. They are found in bread, cereals, and sugar. They are the most quickly digested nutrients, so if we need a sudden burst of energy, like first thing in the morning, foods rich in carbohydrates are the best to eat.

FAT
Fat is another source of energy. It is the easiest nutrient to store, and we need a certain amount of fat to protect our internal organs and bones and to keep us warm. It is, however, the slowest nutrient to be digested. This means it is easy to eat more than we need, and too much fat can make us overweight. Fat is found in butter, oil, margarine, meat, cheese, eggs, peanuts, and chocolate.

VITAMINS
Vitamins are very important nutrients because they release the energy we need from food. There are about 20 different vitamins, and we need a little of all of them to be fit and healthy. The most important ones are:

Vitamin A This helps us grow and gives us healthy skin and eyesight. It is found in fish, liver, milk, cheese, carrots, tomatoes, and green leafy vegetables.

Vitamin B Group There are about 12 different types of vitamin B, and they do a variety of jobs, such as making healthy blood, hair, skin, and nerves. They are found in meat, eggs, bread, cereals, and vegetables.

Vitamin C We need this vitamin to give us healthy blood and skin and to help with healing. It is found in citrus fruit (oranges, lemons, and limes, etc.), soft fruit (strawberries, etc.), potatoes, green vegetables, sweet peppers, and tomatoes.

Vitamin D This gives us strong bones and good teeth. Sunshine is one source of vitamin D, but in the winter we need to get extra from food. It is found in eggs, butter, milk, and oily fish.

Vitamin E This vitamin carries oxygen around our body and protects

important chemicals. It is found in nuts, green leafy vegetables, whole wheat bread, and cereals.

MINERALS
We need small amounts of about 20 different minerals to work with vitamins and proteins. The most important minerals are calcium, iron, salt, potassium, magnesium, iodine, manganese, and zinc. A diet containing milk, nuts, cereals, vegetables, fish, and eggs will give you plenty of these minerals.

FIBER
We also need fiber in our diet, although it does not actually nourish us in any way. We cannot digest fiber or break it down, but it helps us digest the food we eat. Most fiber comes from a material called cellulose, found in plants. So, fresh and whole foods contain the best supply. Try to eat whole wheat pasta and bread, brown rice, and potatoes, vegetables, and fruit with the skins left on.

RUMBLE-TUMBLE EGGS

This quick and easy breakfast dish is made from beaten eggs stir-fried with bacon, mushrooms, and onions. Other ingredients such as scallions, chopped green or red sweet peppers, ham, or corn can be used if you prefer. Pile portions on plates and serve with toast triangles and tomato slices or wedges. Serves 4.

YOU WILL NEED

1 medium onion
6 slices Canadian bacon
8 small mushrooms
6 large eggs
Salt and pepper
2 tablespoons butter
4 small tomatoes
4 to 6 slices bread

SAFETY TIP: *Make sure a grown-up helps you when using a sharp knife and the stove top.*

1 Peel and slice the onion and then carefully chop it into small pieces. Remove the rind (if any) from the bacon and cut into thin strips. Wipe the mushrooms clean and slice them thinly from the stems downward.

2 Break the eggs into a bowl and beat them with a fork until the yolks and whites are blended. Season with pinches of salt and a little pepper. Cut the tomatoes in slices or wedges. Toast the bread, trim off the crusts, and cut in triangles.

3 Melt the butter in a frying pan over low heat and cook the onion until it is transparent. Add the bacon and the mushrooms and fry for a few minutes, until cooked, stirring all the time with a wooden fork or spatula.

4 Turn up the heat a little and pour the egg mixture into the pan. Stir briskly with the wooden fork to break up the eggs into small pieces as they set and to distribute the bacon mixture evenly. When the eggs are cooked, pile on a serving platter. Put the toast around the eggs and the tomatoes on top.

MUNCHY CEREAL

A healthful and nutritious cereal, fruit, and nut breakfast to suit all tastes. Serve yourself, and your friends, all your favorite ingredients topped with milk, yogurt, honey, or even fruit juice.

YOU WILL NEED

Walnuts and apple
Lemon juice
Dried apricots and
  pitted prunes
Golden raisins and dried
  banana slices
Sliced almonds and oats
Bran flakes and
  crunchy cereal
Honey and plain
  yogurt
Milk

SAFETY TIP: *Make sure a grown-up helps you when using a sharp knife.*

1 Break the walnuts into small pieces and put into a small serving dish.

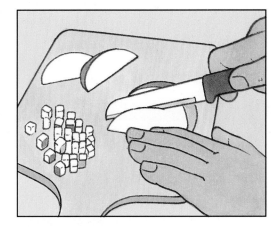

2 Wash the apple and cut into quarters. Remove the stem and core. Chop into small cubes and put in a serving dish. Sprinkle a little lemon juice over the apple to stop it from going brown.

3 Use a knife and a chopping board to cut the dried apricots and prunes into small pieces.

4 Put all the remaining ingredients (except the milk) in separate serving dishes. Pour the milk into a pitcher. Arrange everything on the table ready to serve.

SWEET CREPES

Crepes are great fun to make, and they taste delicious. For a special breakfast treat, pile them high and pour maple syrup over them. Or roll the crepes up and serve with lemon juice and sugar. Serves 4.

1 Sift the flour and salt into a mixing bowl. Break the eggs into the center of the flour. Whisk the flour, salt, and eggs together.

SAFETY TIP: *Make sure a grown-up helps you when using the stove top and oven.*

2 Mix the milk and water together, then gradually stir into the flour mixture. Whisk together until the batter is smooth.

3 Heat a little butter in the frying pan, and when it melts, put in about 2 tablespoons of the batter. Tip the pan quickly so that the batter spreads evenly and thinly over the pan. Cook for about 1 minute, until golden.

4 Turn the crepe over with a spatula and cook the other side. Tip out onto a large plate and sprinkle with a teaspoon each of sugar and lemon juice.

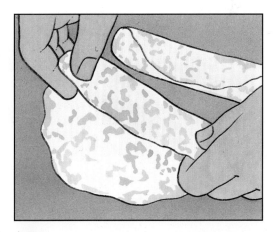

YOU WILL NEED

½ cup all-purpose flour
Pinch of salt
2 eggs
1 cup milk
⅓ cup water
Butter for cooking
Sugar
Lemon juice

5 Starting at one side, roll up the crepe and then transfer it to the serving dish. Sprinkle with lemon juice and a little more sugar. Keep warm in a low oven or cover with a lid.

FRANKFURTER FACES

YOU WILL NEED

2 frankfurters
Cooking oil
1 medium tomato
Curly lettuce leaves
1 mushroom
Capers
Stuffed olives
Finger rolls

Invite some friends over for lunch and try making these fun frankfurter faces. Follow the recipe shown here, or use different ingredients such as celery, cucumber, ham, and red or green sweet peppers to make different faces or other patterns. Serves 1.

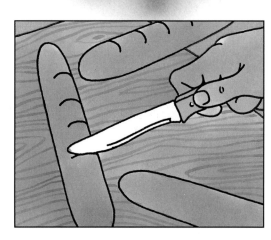

1 Using a small kitchen knife, make crosswise cuts along the length of each frankfurter. This will make the frankfurters bend as you cook them. Heat a little cooking oil in a frying pan and cook the frankfurters until they are golden brown all over.

2 Cut a zigzag line around the tomato. Slice into the tomato to separate the halves. Use these as the eyes.

3 Lay the 2 frankfurters on a plate for the mouth. Add the lettuce leaves for the hair. Finish the face with the other vegetables and garnishes, as shown.

4 Or, for a tasty snack, make 2 parallel cuts in a roll. Push a frankfurter into each cut and add tomato and lettuce.

BAKED POTATOES

Baked potatoes go well with lots of dishes, such as casseroles and broiled meat, but if you add various fillings, hot and cold, they become a meal on their own!

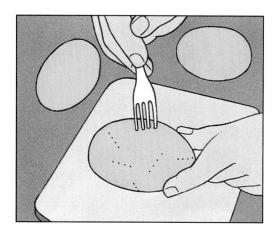

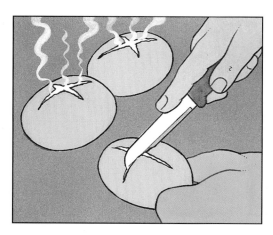

1 Wash and dry the potatoes. Prick them all over with a fork. Preheat the oven to 425° F. Put in the potatoes and cook for about 1 hour.

YOU WILL NEED

Large potatoes,
  1 for each person
Butter
Salt and pepper

Fillings
Grated Cheddar cheese and
  baked beans
Cooked, diced chicken and
  corn
Tuna, mayonnaise, scallion

2 Wearing oven gloves, test the potatoes by squeezing them gently. When they feel slightly soft, take them out of the oven and cut a cross in the top of each. Squeeze the sides gently to open up the cuts.

SAFETY TIP: *Make sure a grown-up helps you when using a sharp knife and the oven.*

3 Carefully spoon out the soft potato and put it in a shallow dish. Try not to tear the potato skin.

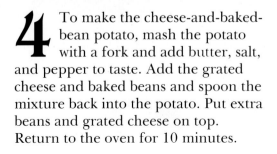

4 To make the cheese-and-baked-bean potato, mash the potato with a fork and add butter, salt, and pepper to taste. Add the grated cheese and baked beans and spoon the mixture back into the potato. Put extra beans and grated cheese on top. Return to the oven for 10 minutes.

5 To make the chicken-and-corn potato, cut the cooked potato in half lengthways. Scoop out the potato and mix with cooked chicken and corn. Spoon the mixture back into the potato skins and return to the oven for 10 minutes.

6 If you prefer a cold filling, let the potato cool a little. Mix tuna, mayonnaise, and chopped scallion together. Cut a cross in the top of the potato and pile the filling on top.

TANGY KABOBS

Have a great time making your own kabobs. They're best cooked outdoors on the barbecue grill, but a broiler will do nearly as well. It's hard work preparing all the different ingredients, but it's fun choosing your favorite foods to thread on a skewer and cook.

1 Using a sharp knife, trim off any fat from the meat and cut it into small cubes about 1 inch square. Put each type of meat in a separate dish. Keep whole the cocktail franks, cherry tomatoes, and mushrooms. Put them all in separate dishes.

YOU WILL NEED

Steak, about 1 inch thick
Chicken breasts
Pork cutlet
Cocktail franks
Cherry tomatoes
Tiny white mushrooms
Red, yellow, and green
  sweet peppers
1 large onion
2 or 3 small zucchini
Olive oil

4 To make up the kabobs, push the ingredients onto wooden skewers, alternating the different meats and vegetables. Brush with a little olive oil and broil for 5 to 6 minutes, turning often.

3 Peel the onion and cut in quarters. Separate the layers of onion and cut any large pieces in half. Slice the zucchini thick. Put in dishes.

SAFETY TIP: *Make sure a grown-up helps you when using a sharp knife and the broiler.*

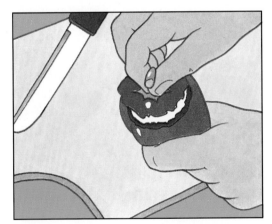

2 Cut out the stalks and seed sections from the sweet peppers. Cut the peppers into small squares and put in a dish.

TANDOORI CHICKEN

Make this favorite Indian dish at home, but don't forget to start by making the spicy yogurt marinade the day before. Leave the chicken to soak in the marinade overnight so that it absorbs the flavors. Next day, bake it in the oven. Serve with the yogurt-mint dressing and rice.
Serves 4.

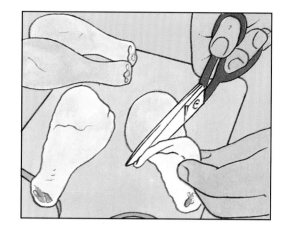

1 Make the marinade the day before you want to eat this dish. Mix the yogurt, spices, oil, lemon juice, and salt and pepper in a bowl. Remove the skin from the chicken drumsticks (use kitchen scissors to help you) and place them in one layer in a flat dish.

YOU WILL NEED

⅔ cup plain yogurt
3 teaspoons tandoori spices
1 tablespoon oil
2 teaspoons lemon juice
Salt and pepper
8 chicken drumsticks

Dressing
2 tablespoons chopped fresh mint
⅔ cup plain yogurt
1 teaspoon lemon juice

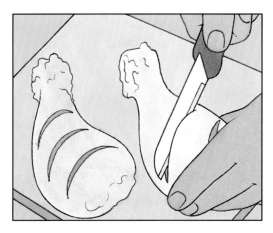

2 Using a kitchen knife, make slits in the chicken. This allows the marinade to really soak in.

4 The next day, make the dressing. Chop the mint leaves very fine and add to the yogurt. Mix in the lemon juice and some salt and pepper, and leave for 1 hour to allow all the flavors to blend.

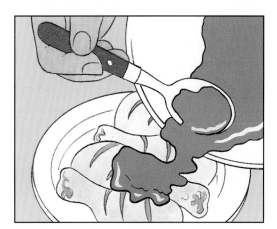

3 Pour the marinade over the chicken drumsticks. Cover and leave in the refrigerator overnight.

5 Preheat the oven to 475° F. Put the chicken in a roasting pan in one layer and bake in the oven for about 20 minutes. Serve with the dressing on the side.

SAFETY TIP: *Make sure a grown-up helps you when using a sharp knife and the oven.*

TASTY BURGERS

This recipe shows you how to make really delicious burgers. You won't believe how much better they are than plain hamburger patties. Cook them under the broiler or on a barbecue grill, and serve in sesame-seed buns with all the trimmings. Makes 8.

1 Peel and chop the onion very fine. Mix the beef and bread crumbs in a large bowl and add the onion. Mix well.

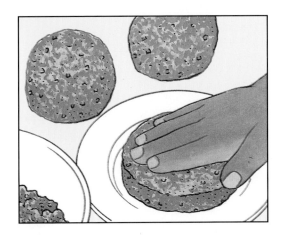

2 Beat the egg and mix in the tomato sauce, mustard, and salt and pepper. Add this mixture to the meat and mix well.

3 Divide the mixture into 8 equal portions. Take a portion in your hand and shape it into a ball. Put it on a flat surface and press down to make a flat burger about 1 inch thick.

4 Cook the burgers for about 4 to 6 minutes on each side. Serve with all your favorite trimmings (such as lettuce, tomato, onion, cucumber or pickle slices) in sesame-seed buns.

SAFETY TIP: *Make sure a grown-up helps you when using a sharp knife and the broiler.*

YOU WILL NEED

1 medium onion
2 pounds ground beef
$\frac{1}{3}$ cup fresh bread crumbs
1 egg
2 tablespoons tomato sauce
1 teaspoon French mustard
1 teaspoon salt
Pepper
8 sesame-seed buns

PERFECT PASTA

Learn to cook pasta perfectly every time. The secrets are don't overcook it, use lots of boiling water, add a few drops of olive oil to stop it sticking together, and rinse it well when cooked. To go with the pasta, make a delicious tomato and herb sauce. Serves 4.

SAFETY TIP: *Make sure a grown-up helps you when using a sharp knife and the stove top.*

1 To make the sauce, chop the onion into small pieces and fry in the oil with the garlic and salt and pepper.

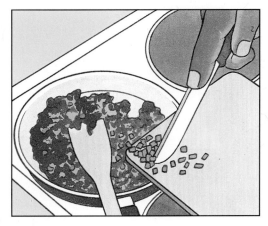

2 Add the tomatoes and cook briskly for a few minutes to reduce the juice. Add chopped basil and sugar to the tomato sauce. Turn off the heat.

3 Boil plenty of water in a large saucepan and add the salt and oil. Put in the pasta and stir with a wooden spoon until the water starts to bubble. Lower the heat and cook the pasta for the time suggested on the packet, but test it a short time before. Take out a piece of pasta, cool it, and taste it. It should be just tender when it's cooked.

YOU WILL NEED

1 teaspoon salt
1 tablespoon olive oil
½ cup pasta per person (shells, tagliatelli, spaghetti)
Grated Parmesan cheese, to sprinkle on top

Tomato and herb sauce
1 onion
2 tablespoons olive oil
1 teaspoon garlic puree
Salt and pepper
1 (15-ounce) can chopped tomatoes
1 tablespoon chopped fresh basil
Pinch of sugar

4 Drain the pasta in a colander and rinse with hot water. Pour on a little oil and toss. Serve hot with the tomato sauce. Sprinkle with Parmesan cheese.

PATTERNED PIZZA

Have fun making this delicious pizza. Use your imagination and a selection of tasty ingredients to create different patterns and flavors. It's easy to make and easy to eat! Serves 2.

YOU WILL NEED

7-inch pizza dough base
(homemade or bought)
Tomato puree
Mozzarella cheese, sliced
Red, green, and yellow
    sweet peppers
Tomatoes
Mushrooms
Scallions
Stuffed olives
Cooking oil

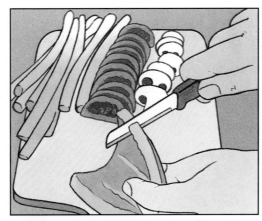

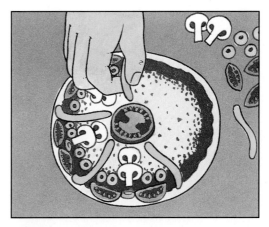

1 Preheat the oven to 400° F. Spread the pizza dough base thickly with tomato puree and then place the slices of mozzarella cheese over the top.

2 Prepare all the toppings ready to use on the pizza. Slice the peppers into long strips. Cut the tomatoes into circles and slice the mushrooms thin from the stalk downward. Slice the scallions at a slanting angle. Cut the olives into tiny circles.

3 Arrange your favorite ingredients on your pizza. Start with something like a tomato circle in the center and then place 5 or 6 pieces of pepper spread out like the spokes of a wheel. Next decorate the edge and fill in the spaces with an attractive mix of toppings.

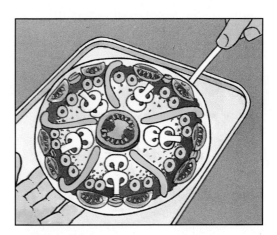

4 Spread a little oil on a baking sheet to prevent the pizza from sticking. Lift the decorated pizza carefully onto the sheet and bake in the oven for about 15 minutes. Serve the pizza whole or in slices.

SAFETY TIP: *Make sure a grown-up helps you when using a sharp knife and the oven.*

EXOTIC FRUIT SALAD

You can use all your favorite fruits in this delicious salad, plus a few that you haven't tried before. Choose about five varieties of fruit from this selection: mangoes, kiwifruit, star fruit, oranges, melons, peaches, nectarines, apples, cherries, papaya, strawberries, grapes, and pineapples.
Serves 4.

YOU WILL NEED
½ cup sugar
½ pint water
Juice of 1 lemon or 1 lime
About 5 types of fruit,
  including half a melon
  or pineapple

1 First make the syrup. Put the sugar and water into a saucepan and stir over low heat until the sugar dissolves. Boil for 2 minutes and leave to cool in a bowl.

2 Cut the lemon or lime in half and squeeze out the juice with the lemon squeezer. Remove any seeds. Add the juice to the syrup.

4 Peel the oranges and remove the seeds. Separate the orange segments. Remove the skin from the kiwifruit and slice as shown.

3 Wash and chop up all the fruit into small pieces. You can leave the skin on the apples, cherries, and grapes, but remove the seeds or pits. The rest of the fruit should be peeled and sliced into small pieces.

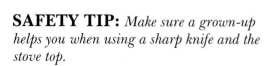

SAFETY TIP: *Make sure a grown-up helps you when using a sharp knife and the stove top.*

5 Cut the melon in half and scoop out the fruit. The best way to do this is with a melon baller. Put all the pieces of fruit in a bowl and pour the syrup over.

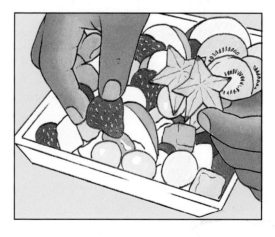

6 Try to catch any juice that runs from the fruit and add this to the syrup with all the fruit pieces. Decorate with slices of star fruit and strawberry. Cover with plastic wrap and chill in the refrigerator for about 1 hour.

SHORTBREAD

Real butter shortbread is one of the most delicious treats to serve with tea or for a party dessert. Cut the dough into fun animal shapes before baking, or divide the shortbread into segments after it has been cooked. Makes 8 cookies.

1 Sift the flour into a bowl and mix in the sugar. Work the soft butter into the mixture with your fingertips. Preheat the oven to 325° F.

2 Knead the mixture well until the dough holds together, and then press it into a greased cake pan or pie pan. Prick the surface with a fork.

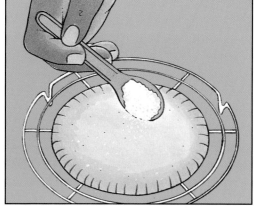

3 Bake in the oven for about 45 minutes, or until the shortbread is firm. Turn it out of the pan onto a wire rack and leave to cool. Sprinkle with confectioner's sugar.

4 Mark the segments with a knife while the shortbread is still warm. Separate the segments when the shortbread has cooled.

YOU WILL NEED

¾ cup all-purpose flour
¼ cup sugar
½ cup butter, softened
Butter to grease pan
Confectioner's sugar

SAFETY TIP: *Make sure a grown-up helps you when using the oven.*

CUPCAKES

Use this delicious cake recipe to make one large cake or lots of small cupcakes. Makes 12 cupcakes.

2 Beat the eggs in a small bowl and gradually add to the butter-sugar mixture, a little at a time. Beat well to blend evenly.

YOU WILL NEED

½ cup butter, softened
½ cup sugar
2 eggs
½ cup self-rising flour

Glacé icing
½ cup confectioner's sugar
Cold water

Cake decorations

1 Preheat the oven to 375° F. In a mixing bowl, cream together the butter and the sugar, using a wooden spoon. Beat well until the mixture is pale and fluffy.

3 Sift the flour and add to the mixture. Fold it in lightly with a metal spoon.

4 Put the bake cups on a baking tray and spoon in the mixture. Bake near the top of the oven for about 10 to 12 minutes. Do not open the oven door or the cakes will sink!

SAFETY TIP: *Make sure a grown-up helps you when using the oven.*

5 Make the glacé icing by mixing the confectioner's sugar in a bowl with the water. Add the water a little at a time, until the icing is thick enough to coat the back of a spoon. Use a spatula to smooth the icing on top of the cakes. Decorate with sprinkles or any cake decoration you like.

CHOCOLATE CAKE

This is a variation on the basic cake recipe. It's a really delicious chocolate cake with a delectable mocha (that's coffee and chocolate) filling. The top has been decorated by sprinkling confectioner's sugar through a paper doily. If this looks a bit too pretty for your liking, why not try a lattice of paper strips to give a striped or checked effect?

1 Make up the basic cake mixture as shown on page 34, but sift the cocoa powder in with the flour so that the color and flavor are even.

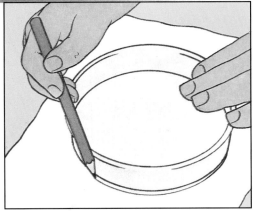

2 Place two 8-inch cake pans on wax paper and draw around them. Cut out the circles. Grease the pans with butter and line them with the circles.

3 Carefully divide the mixture equally into both pans and smooth the tops with a spatula to ensure evenness. Bake near the top of the oven for 20 minutes at 375° F. Leave to cool on a wire tray.

4 While the cake is baking, make the mocha filling. Put the butter in a bowl and sift in the sugar and cocoa powder. Add the coffee extract and blend well together. If the filling is too stiff, add a little milk; it should be smooth and light in texture. Spread the filling on one cake and put the other cake on top. Choose the cake with the smoothest surface to go on top.

SAFETY TIP: *Make sure a grown-up helps you when using the oven.*

5 Put the confectioner's sugar in a sifter so that it falls in a fine mist rather than sudden lumps. Place a paper doily on top of the cake and sprinkle over the confectioner's sugar. Remove the doily carefully.

YOU WILL NEED

½ cup butter, softened
½ cup sugar
2 eggs
½ cup self-rising flour
1 tablespoon cocoa powder

Mocha filling

¼ cup butter
½ cup confectioner's sugar
1 tablespoon cocoa powder
1 teaspoon coffee extract
1 tablespoon milk (about)

Confectioner's sugar to decorate

JELLY TARTS

Once you can make piecrust pastry, used here for these tasty jelly tarts, you will be able to try lots of other delicious pastry recipes. Here are a few simple tips to remember: handle the dough as little as possible, use the margarine at room temperature, keep your hands cool, and use ice water for mixing. Makes 12.

YOU WILL NEED

½ cup all-purpose flour
Pinch of salt
2 tablespoons
    margarine
2 tablespoons
    vegetable
    shortening
Ice water
Strawberry
    or apricot jelly

1 Sift the flour and salt into a large mixing bowl. Cut the margarine and shortening into little bits and drop them into the flour. Mix with a knife.

2 Rub the flour mixture together with your fingers until it looks like bread crumbs.

3 Sprinkle 2 tablespoons ice water into the mixture. Stir in quickly with a spatula. Add more water, if necessary. Now with your hands form the dough into a ball that leaves the bowl clean. Wrap the pastry in plastic wrap and leave in the refrigerator for 30 minutes; this makes it easier to roll out. Preheat the oven to 375° F.

4 Sprinkle flour on the work surface and the rolling pin. Gently roll out the dough to ⅛ inch thick. Cut the pastry into circles with the cutter and put into tart tins or muffin pans.

5 Put 1 teaspoon jelly into each tart and bake in the oven for about 15 minutes, until the pastry is golden.

SAFETY TIP: *Make sure a grown-up helps you when using the oven.*

TOASTED SANDWICHES

Hot toasted sandwiches make a scrumptious party snack. Try making a selection with different fillings, such as cheese, ham, and tomato or cooked bacon and mushrooms. Serve them with a side salad for a more substantial meal. (See the suggestions in Step 5.)

YOU WILL NEED

Butter for frying
4 slices Canadian bacon
¼ cup sliced mushrooms
4 slices white bread
¼ cup grated Cheddar cheese or cheese slices
1 slice ham
1 tomato, sliced
Parsley for garnish

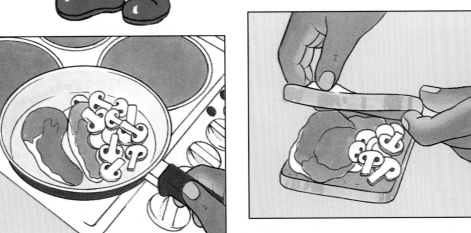

1 To make the bacon and mushroom sandwich, heat a little butter in a frying pan over low heat. Add the bacon and mushrooms and cook for about 4 minutes. Remove with a spatula and drain on paper towels.

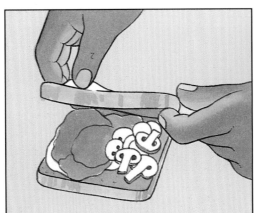

2 Lightly toast one side of the 2 slices of bread. Put the bacon and mushrooms on the toasted side of one slice of bread. Put the second slice of bread, toasted side down, on top to make a sandwich. Brown the outside under the broiler.

3 To make the cheese, ham, and tomato sandwich, lightly toast one side of the 2 slices of bread. Top the bread with the cheese and melt under the broiler.

5 Cut the sandwiches into triangles, and remove the crusts if you wish. Serve with a side salad of sliced tomatoes with olive oil and black pepper, or shredded lettuce with a vinaigrette dressing.

4 Add slices of ham and tomato to the melted cheese. Put the second slice of bread, toasted side down, on top to make a sandwich. Brown the outside under the broiler, as before.

SAFETY TIP: *Make sure a grown-up helps you when using the broiler and the stove top.*

PARTY SANDWICHES

These "double-decker" sandwiches are great for parties. They should always be made with very thinly sliced bread and cut into small triangles, oblongs, or other small shapes. Trim off the crusts to show the fillings and the different kinds of bread.

1 Soften the butter so that it's easy to spread. Butter 4 slices of dark bread—whole wheat, whole-grain, or pumpernickel—on one side and 2 slices of white bread on both sides. You will need 2 slices of dark bread and 1 slice of white bread for each sandwich.

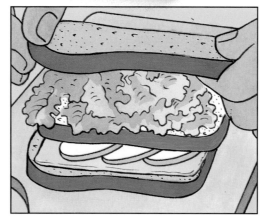

2 For the Edam cheese, apple, and lettuce sandwich, arrange the cheese and apple slices on 1 slice of dark bread. Cover with the white slice and arrange the lettuce leaves on top. Top with dark bread, buttered side down.

3 To make the tuna, mayonnaise, and cucumber sandwich, mix the tuna and mayonnaise together in a bowl. Spread the mixture on a slice of dark bread and cover with a slice of white bread, buttered on both sides. Arrange slices of cucumber on top and cover with a slice of dark bread.

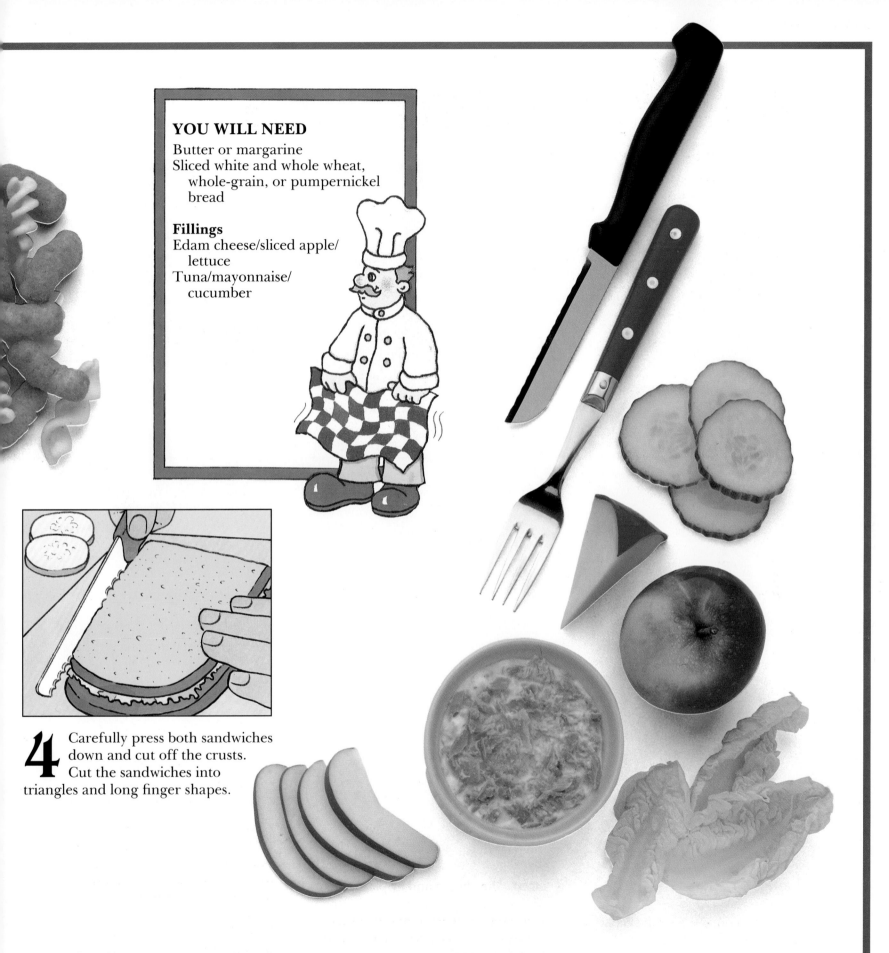

YOU WILL NEED

Butter or margarine
Sliced white and whole wheat,
   whole-grain, or pumpernickel
   bread

Fillings
Edam cheese/sliced apple/
   lettuce
Tuna/mayonnaise/
   cucumber

4 Carefully press both sandwiches
down and cut off the crusts.
Cut the sandwiches into
triangles and long finger shapes.

SAFETY TIP: *Make sure a grown-up helps you when using a sharp knife.*

SAUSAGE AND APPLE PARCELS

Use your pastry-making skills to make these tasty, savory parcels. Decorate them with pastry leaves and serve them cold as a party snack, or eat them hot with vegetables as a main meal. Make the pastry following the method used for jelly tarts on page 38, but double the ingredients. Makes 4.

YOU WILL NEED

2 recipes piecrust pastry
 (page 38)
1 cup pork sausage meat
½ cup fresh bread crumbs
1 small onion
1 egg, beaten
Salt and pepper
Pinch of mixed herbs
1 large tart apple
Milk to glaze

 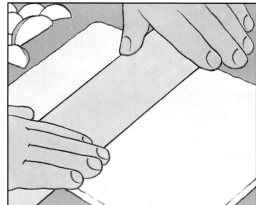

1 Make the pastry dough following the instructions on pages 38 and 39. Mix the sausage meat with the bread crumbs. Peel and chop the onion and add to the sausage with the beaten egg and seasonings.

2 Peel, core, and thickly slice the apple. Roll out the pastry dough on a floured surface and cut out 4 squares. Divide the sausage mix into 4 portions.

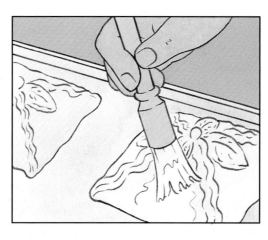

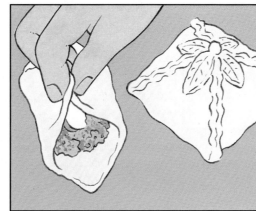

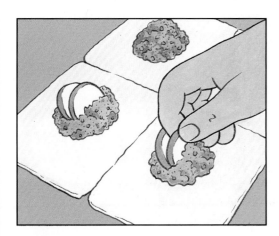

5 Make up the rest of the parcels in the same way, garnish with leaves made out of the leftover pastry, and brush with milk to glaze. Put them on a baking sheet and bake in the oven for 15 minutes, until golden brown.

4 Using a pastry brush, paint the edges of the dough with milk, fold up the corners to meet at the top, and pinch along to seal.

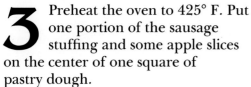

3 Preheat the oven to 425° F. Put one portion of the sausage stuffing and some apple slices on the center of one square of pastry dough.

SAFETY TIP: *Make sure a grown-up helps you when using a sharp knife and the oven.*

CEREAL CAKES

These cakes are really easy to make and need very little cooking. They're just cereals mixed with either melted chocolate or simple caramel made with butter and syrup. If you add chopped nuts or fruit, it makes them even nicer. Makes 12.

3 For the crunchy cakes, melt the butter and syrup in the saucepan and cook gently for about 5 minutes, stirring occasionally.

1 For the chocolate-covered cakes, break the chocolate into small pieces and put in a bowl. Place the bowl over a saucepan of boiling water and leave until the chocolate has completely softened.

2 Remove the bowl of chocolate from the saucepan. Add your chosen cereal and stir carefully until it is well covered with chocolate. Spoon into paper bake cups and leave for about an hour to set.

YOU WILL NEED
Chocolate Crispies
⅓ cup puffed rice
½ cup semisweet chocolate

Nutty Flake Crunch
⅓ cup butter
3 tablespoons light corn syrup
⅓ cup bran flakes
½ cup chopped mixed nuts
Fruity Crunch
⅓ cup butter
3 tablespoons light corn syrup
⅓ cup corn flakes
⅓ cup chopped candied fruit

4 Remove from the heat and stir in the cereals and nuts or fruit. Line a baking sheet with wax paper and pour in the mixture. Press it down flat.

5 Leave to set for about a half hour; then mark sections with a knife. When it is quite cool, remove from the sheet, break into segments, and serve.

SWEET AND SAVORY POPCORN

Re-create the magic of the movie theater with a cone of popcorn to nibble as you watch a video. The recipe shows you how to pop the corn quickly and safely, and how to add butter and salt or whip up a crunchy candy topping.

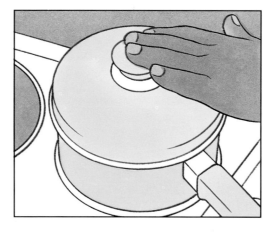

3 When there has been no sound for about a minute, turn off the heat and remove the lid. Tip the corn into a dish and pick out any unpopped kernels.

2 After a few minutes you will hear the corn beginning to pop. Don't take off the lid yet! Lift the pan from time to time and shake gently to speed up the popping.

1 Put about two handfuls of corn in a saucepan so that it just covers the bottom of the pan. Put the lid on and heat gently.

SAFETY TIP: *Make sure a grown-up helps you when using the stove top.*

4 For the savory topping, melt about 2 tablespoons butter in a small saucepan. Drizzle this over the corn and sprinkle on a little salt to taste. Mix well.

YOU WILL NEED
Popping corn

Savory topping
2 tablespoons butter
Salt

Sweet topping
1/3 cup butter
3 tablespoons
  light corn syrup

5 For the sweet topping, cook the butter and syrup in a small pan over low heat. It should bubble for about 5 minutes.

6 Pour this mixture over the corn, mix well, and spread out the corn so that it doesn't stick together. Leave to set.

FRUITY COCKTAILS

These delicious fruity cocktails are refreshing on a hot summer's day. They will also go down very well at a summer party. Add lots of ice cubes and decorate with fruit and colorful cocktail umbrellas and straws for a really special treat. Each of the recipes here makes one cocktail.

1 To make a Tropical Sunrise, pour ice-cold orange or tropical fruit juice into a tall glass, and then gently add a little Grenadine syrup. This will sink to the bottom of the drink, giving the sunrise effect. Decorate the cocktail with slices of orange and lemon.

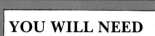

2 For the Honey Lemonade, thinly peel the rind from the lemon. Put the rind in a bowl and add the honey and sugar. Pour in the 1 cup boiling water. Leave to cool. Squeeze the juice from the lemon and add to the liquid. Strain and pour into a glass.

YOU WILL NEED

Tropical Sunrise
Orange or tropical fruit juice
Grenadine syrup
Slices of orange and lemon

Honey Lemonade
1 lemon
1 tablespoon honey
1 tablespoon sugar
1 cup boiling water

Dark Delight
Black cherry juice
Cola
Cherries

Blue Lagoon
Blue food coloring
Lemon-lime seltzer
Slices of lemon,
    lime, and kiwifruit

3 To make a Dark Delight, put several cubes of ice in a tall tumbler. Pour in some black cherry juice and carefully add cola until you reach the top of the glass. Decorate with cherries.

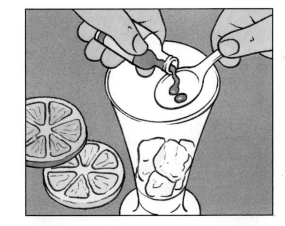

4 For a Blue Lagoon, half fill a glass with ice cubes. Carefully add 2 or 3 drops of blue food coloring and fill up with lemon-lime seltzer. Decorate with slices of lemon, lime, and kiwifruit.

MILK SHAKES

Milk shakes are wonderfully refreshing and nourishing, too. Just one of these shakes with a sandwich, some cookies, or fresh fruit will make a perfect quick snack, whatever you're doing. If you are throwing a party, serve the shakes in tall attractive glasses with colorful straws and decorations. Each of the recipes here makes one milk shake.

2 Whisk in the milk and ice cream until it is frothy. Pour into a glass and sprinkle on the grated chocolate.

1 For the Rich Chocolate Shake, dissolve the cocoa powder and the sugar in a bowl or measuring cup with a little hot water. Stir well to blend.

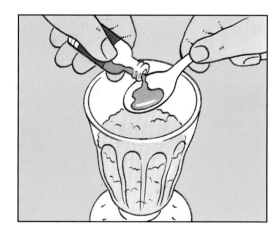

3 To make the Milky Mint, whisk all the ingredients together, using about 3 drops food coloring and ½ teaspoon peppermint extract. Add a little sugar if you wish.

4 For the Continental Coffee, pour the hot water onto the coffee granules, add the sugar, and mix in a bowl until completely dissolved. Put 4 ice cubes in a glass and add the coffee mixture. Pour the milk into the glass. Do not stir this milk shake. Sprinkle some grated chocolate on the top if you wish.

YOU WILL NEED

Rich Chocolate Shake
1 teaspoon cocoa powder
1 teaspoon sugar
1 cup milk
A scoop of chocolate
   ice cream
Grated chocolate

Milky Mint
1 cup milk
A scoop of mint
   chocolate-chip ice cream
Green food coloring
Peppermint extract

Continental Coffee
½ cup hot water
1 teaspoon instant
   coffee granules
2 teaspoons sugar
⅔ cup milk

FEAST FOR FOUR

Once you have mastered some of the recipes in this book, why not try making a complete three-course meal? On the following pages we have suggested a delicious menu for you to make for your friends or family. Most of the work can be done in advance to give you time to serve the food in style and enjoy eating it, too!

MENU

Appetizer
Egg and Shrimp Nests
•
Main Course
Chicken and Vegetable Bake
Scalloped Potatoes
•
Dessert
Meringue Fruit Tart

EGG AND SHRIMP NESTS

A favorite way to start a meal is with this tasty appetizer of chopped hard-boiled egg mixed with shrimp in a seafood sauce. Garnish with tiny triangles of whole wheat bread and butter. Serves 4.

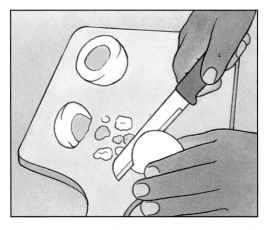

1 Put the eggs in a small saucepan and pour in enough cold water to cover them. Over high heat, bring to a boil and then reduce the heat to simmer for 10 minutes. Remove the pan from the heat and stand in cold water to cool. Peel off the shells and chop the eggs.

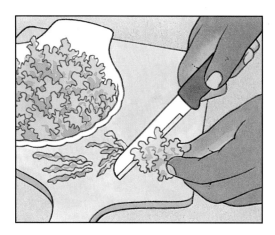

2 Wash and dry the lettuce leaves and cut into shreds. Put in the bottom of 4 individual dishes to make nests for the cocktails.

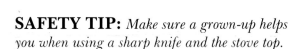

SAFETY TIP: *Make sure a grown-up helps you when using a sharp knife and the stove top.*

3 To make the seafood sauce, mix all the sauce ingredients together in a dish and stir well. Add the shrimp and the chopped egg and mix gently.

4 Divide the shrimp mixture among the 4 dishes and decorate with slices of lemon and a sprinkling of cayenne pepper.

YOU WILL NEED

2 eggs
Lettuce leaves
¾ cup peeled fresh shrimp

Seafood sauce
4 tablespoons mayonnaise
1 tablespoon tomato
    catsup
1 tablespoon plain yogurt
1 teaspoon lemon juice
Dash of Worcestershire
    sauce
Cayenne pepper
Salt and pepper

Lemon slices
Cayenne pepper

YOU WILL NEED

2 tablespoons all-purpose flour
Salt and pepper
1 teaspoon mixed herbs
4 chicken portions, skinned
1 large onion
4 slices bacon
1 tablespoon vegetable oil
4 large carrots
2 small parsnips
2 stalks celery
2 cups chicken stock
   made from a stock cube
½ cup small white
   mushrooms

CHICKEN AND VEGETABLE BAKE

This delicious casserole combines the vegetables and the meat in a tasty sauce. Serve it straight from the oven in an earthenware dish. Teamed with the scalloped potatoes (page 60), it makes a substantial and impressive main course. Serves 4.

1 Mix the flour, salt, pepper, and herbs on a plate. Roll the chicken portions in it to coat them completely. (Do not throw away any leftover seasoned flour—you will use it in Step 3.)

SAFETY TIP: *Make sure a grown-up helps you when using a sharp knife, the stove top, and the oven.*

2 Chop the onion and bacon. Heat the oil in a frying pan over medium heat. Add the onion and bacon and cook gently. Put in the chicken pieces and brown on all sides. Transfer the chicken to a casserole. Preheat the oven to 325° F.

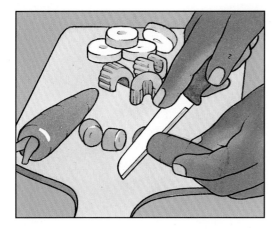

3 Peel and slice the carrots and parsnips and wash and chop the celery. Fry them gently in the pan; then sprinkle on the rest of the seasoned flour and stir constantly for about 2 minutes.

4 Pour in the stock and stir thoroughly, scraping the pan to mix and thicken the sauce. Add the mushrooms.

5 Spoon all the ingredients very carefully into the casserole. Put on the lid and cook in the oven for about 1 hour 20 minutes.

SCALLOPED POTATOES

This delicious potato dish is the perfect partner for the Chicken and Vegetable Bake. Not only do they taste good together, but you can cook them in the same oven, for the same length of time, and serve them both from their cooking dishes. Serves 4.

1 Using the potato peeler, peel the potatoes, and then slice them very thin with a kitchen knife.

SAFETY TIP: *Make sure a grown-up helps you when using a sharp knife and the oven.*

2 Grease the bottom of an ovenproof dish and put in a layer of potatoes. Dot a little butter over them and sprinkle on some salt and pepper.

3 Continue to add layers of potato slices. Sprinkle each layer with salt and pepper and dot with butter.

4 Pour over the milk and add the last of the butter so that the top layer of potatoes will get crunchy when it is cooked. Cook in the oven with the Chicken and Vegetable Bake for about 1 hour 20 minutes.

YOU WILL NEED
2 pounds potatoes
2 tablespoons butter
1 teaspoon salt
Black pepper
1 cup milk

MERINGUE FRUIT TART

What an impressive dessert—you'll hardly believe you made it yourself! A delicious meringue base topped with a layer of whipped cream and whatever fresh fruit you fancy. Try strawberries, raspberries, kiwifruit, or a mixture of them all. Serves 4.

1 Break the eggs into a mixing bowl and carefully lift out the yolks with a spoon. It's very important that the bowl is free from grease and that there is absolutely no yolk mixed in with the whites.

YOU WILL NEED

3 large fresh egg whites
¾ cup sugar
1 cup heavy cream
1½ cups soft fruit, sliced

SAFETY TIP: *Make sure a grown-up helps you when using the oven.*

2 Using a hand or rotary whisk, beat the egg whites until they form soft peaks, then whisk in the sugar a tablespoon at a time. Preheat the oven to 300° F.

4 Make a dip in the center of the meringue and draw up little peaks around the edge with the tip of a fork. Put in the oven and turn the temperature down to 275° F. Cook for 1 hour. Turn off the oven but leave the meringue inside for at least 2 hours or overnight. Remove from the oven and peel off the paper.

5 Using the whisk, whip the cream until it forms soft peaks. Just before serving, spoon the cream into the meringue case and decorate with the sliced fruit.

3 Lay a sheet of wax paper on a baking sheet and carefully spoon the meringue onto it in a circle.

INDEX

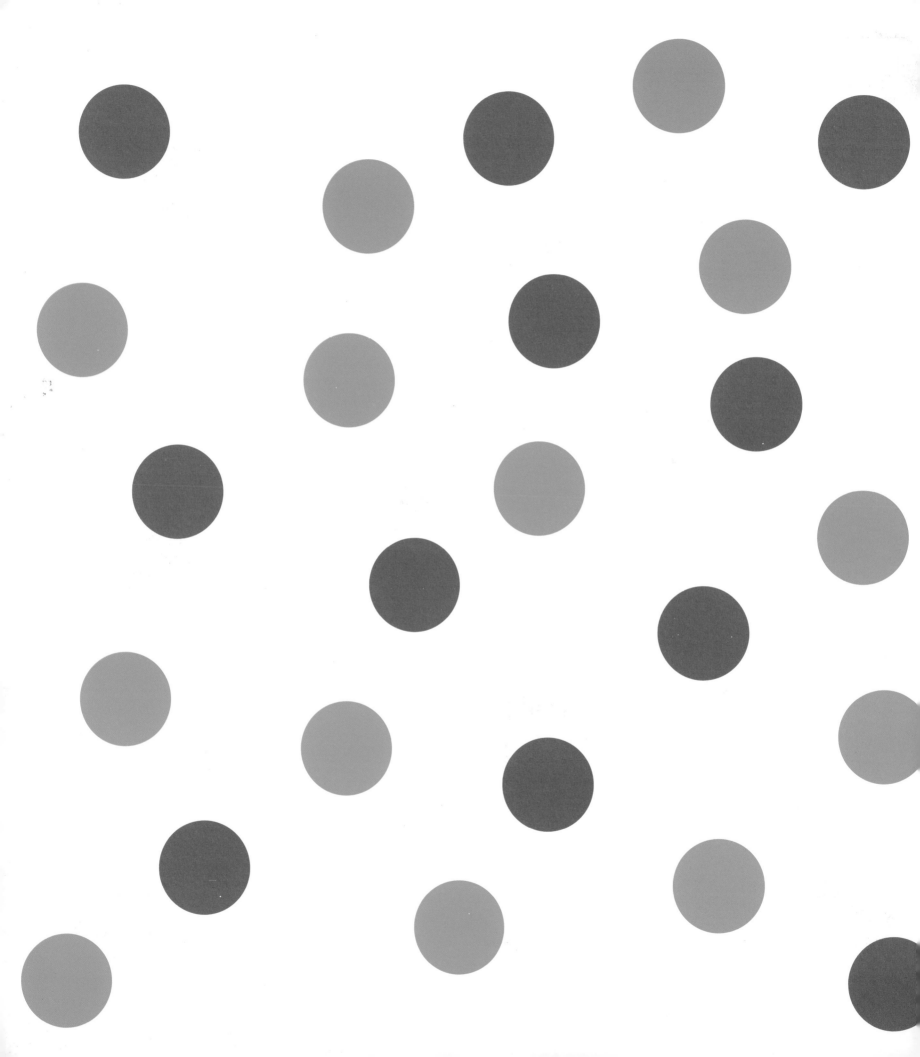